Heidi *was first published as two books, written in German by a Swiss author, Johanna Spyri, who lived in Zurich. This gentle story has since been translated into many different languages and has been popular with children all over the world for more than a century.*

British Library Cataloguing in Publication Data
Ainsworth, Alison
    Heidi.
    I. Title   II. Spyri, Johanna, *1829-1901*   III. Tourret, Pat
    823'.914 [J]
    ISBN 0-7214-1210-6

First edition

Published by Ladybird Books Ltd Loughborough Leicestershire UK
Ladybird Books Inc Auburn Maine 04210 USA
© LADYBIRD BOOKS LTD MCMXC
Printed in England

HEIDI

by Johanna Spyri

retold by Alison Ainsworth
illustrated by Pat Tourret

Ladybird Books

Up to the Alm Uncle

This is the story of a little orphan girl called Heidi, who was so happy and cheerful that she made everyone around her happy too. The story begins one bright sunny day, in the mountains of Switzerland.

Heidi and her Aunt Dete were making their way up a steep path to the cottage where Heidi's grandfather lived. Aunt Dete had looked after Heidi since she was a baby, but now she had a job in a big city called Frankfurt, and she wanted Heidi's grandfather to look after the child.

Heidi didn't know it, but her grandfather was a fierce old man who spoke to no one. The only times he came down from his home on the mountain were when he had goats' cheese to sell in Dorfli, the village in the valley. Everyone called him the Alm Uncle, because the mountain he lived on was called the Alm.

Before Heidi and her aunt reached the cottage, they met a young goatherd called Peter, who was taking his goats to the high pasture. Heidi walked amongst the goats, chattering happily to Peter. The sun shone down from the clear blue sky, and Heidi, who had a thick red shawl tied all around her, began to feel very hot indeed. She unwrapped the shawl, kicked off her heavy walking boots, and skipped along on the soft green grass in her bare feet. She was entranced by her new surroundings. She had never seen anything as beautiful as the mountains before.

At last they reached the Alm Uncle's cottage. The Alm Uncle was sitting outside on a bench, and Heidi went straight up to him.

'Good day, Grandfather!' she said, holding out her hand.

'Well, well, what have we here?' enquired the old man, glaring at Heidi from beneath his bushy eyebrows. Dete explained that she could no longer look after Heidi. Then, as she was rather frightened of the old man, she turned and ran off down the mountain.

At first, the Alm Uncle was cross. After all, he hadn't seen Heidi since she was a baby, and what did he know about looking after little girls? But he could see that Heidi was a bright, happy child, and his old heart softened.

Heidi couldn't wait to explore her new home. The cottage was small but cosy. There was one big room with a fireplace where all the cooking was done. The only furniture was a table and chair, and Grandfather's bed. In one corner stood a ladder. Heidi climbed up the ladder and found herself in a small hayloft. A bale of hay, fresh and sweet-smelling, lay on the floor. From a little window in the roof Heidi could see far down into the valley.

'Oh, Grandfather,' cried Heidi, 'please let me sleep here! It's lovely!'

So Grandfather brought thick sheets and blankets and made a bed in the hay. Then it was time to eat. Supper was a large chunk of cheese, with a thick slice of bread and a bowl of fresh goats' milk, and everything tasted delicious. That night Heidi lay in her soft little bed listening happily to the wind in the pine trees. Soon she was fast asleep, dreaming of goats and mountains.

On the Alm

The next morning Grandfather asked Heidi if she would like to go to the pasture with Peter. Heidi could think of nothing better. Grandfather put a huge piece of cheese and an even bigger piece of bread in Peter's rucksack. 'This is Heidi's lunch,' he explained. Then he gave Peter a wooden bowl. 'This is for Heidi, too,' he said. 'Milk one of the goats and give Heidi two good bowlfuls.'

The two children set off for the high pasture. Peter waved his stick and whistled to keep the goats together. Heidi skipped along at his side,

stopping every now and then to look at the beautiful flowers that grew all around.

When they reached the high pasture, Peter stretched out on the grass, and Heidi sat beside him. The valley lay far below, sparkling in the morning sunshine. The golden sunlight, the fresh breeze and the delicate perfume of the flowers filled Heidi with delight. She wished she could stay there forever.

When it was time to eat, Heidi gave Peter most of her bread and cheese. Peter had never had such a good lunch, as his family were poor and there never seemed to be enough to eat.

The day passed quickly. Suddenly Heidi exclaimed, 'Look, Peter! The mountains are burning! And the sky is on fire, too!' Peter laughed, and said it was like that every evening at sunset. Heidi gasped as the mountains and the sky turned a rosy pink. A moment later, everything was grey, and it was time to return home.

That evening, Heidi asked Grandfather why the mountain had seemed to be on fire.

'That's what the sun does when he says goodnight to the mountains,' he explained.

Once more, Heidi slept peacefully in her little bed of hay, dreaming of pink mountains and flowers.

Peter's grandmother

The weeks passed, and Heidi spent every day on the pasture with Peter and the goats. Her little face shone with health.

Autumn came, and the days grew colder. Instead of going to the pasture with Peter, Heidi watched Grandfather at his carpenter's bench, or helped him to make the delicious goats' cheese.

Then one morning Heidi woke to find the whole Alm covered with snow. Peter could no longer herd the goats. During the winter, he was supposed to go to school. But he wouldn't go, because he hated lessons, and couldn't see the point of learning to read or write.

One evening he came to see Heidi, and told her that his grandmother would like Heidi to visit her. So the next day, Grandfather wrapped Heidi in a warm blanket and took her down the mountain on his big sledge. When they reached Peter's cottage, Grandfather unwrapped Heidi and put her down by the door. Then he pulled the sledge back up the mountain.

Heidi opened the cottage door. It was dark inside, and very shabby. Some of the windows were cracked and there were holes in the roof. In one corner sat an old lady, bent over a spinning wheel.

'Good afternoon, Grandmother!' said Heidi, going over to her. The old lady reached out and touched Heidi's head.

'Is it Heidi?' she asked. After a moment, Heidi realised that the old lady couldn't see at all. She was blind.

Heidi stayed with Grandmother all afternoon, chattering about the mountains and Grandfather. Peter's grandmother had not enjoyed herself so much for a long time.

The next day Heidi visited Grandmother again. This time Grandfather went with her and mended the broken windows. Peter's mother and grandmother were pleased to see him, because it was a long time since he had visited them. They were also thankful to have the windows repaired.

All through the winter, Heidi visited Peter's cottage, and Grandmother's days were no longer as dreary as they had once been.

Two visitors to the Alm

A year went by, and Heidi was eight years old. One sunny spring morning, she was surprised to see an old gentleman dressed in black making his way up to the cottage. It was the pastor. He had come to ask the Alm Uncle to live in the village during the winter, so that Heidi could go to school. But Grandfather was a stubborn old man. He hated the villagers and would have nothing to do with them. The pastor shook his head sadly, and returned to the village.

Later that day, another visitor arrived. This time it was Dete, dressed in fine city clothes. Grandfather was not pleased to see her.

Dete explained that she had come to take Heidi to Frankfurt. She knew of a wealthy businessman who wanted a companion for his invalid daughter, and she thought Heidi would be perfect. She told Grandfather it would be much better for Heidi to live with a good family, where she could learn proper manners and wear fine clothes.

At first, Grandfather was furious, but he knew he couldn't keep Heidi to himself, so, with a heavy heart, he agreed to let her go.

Heidi didn't want to leave Grandfather, but Dete told her that she could come back at once if she didn't like living in Frankfurt. Then she gathered Heidi's clothes together and wrapped them in the red shawl. Heidi wanted to say goodbye to Grandmother, but Dete said they must hurry or they would miss the train. She told Heidi that she could bring back some nice soft white rolls for Grandmother. At once, Heidi brightened, and she started to run down the mountain. She didn't realise that Frankfurt was a long way away, and she couldn't wait to fetch the rolls for Grandmother!

Frankfurt

In a big house in Frankfurt, Clara Sesemann waited impatiently for her new companion to arrive. Clara was twelve years old. She was a delicate child — her legs were so weak that she had to sit in a wheelchair — and she had no brothers or sisters to keep her company. Her father was a kind man, but he was away a great deal on business trips. Clara's mother had died several years before, and the household was looked after by a very strict woman called Fraulein Rottenmeier.

At last Heidi and Dete arrived. When Fraulein Rottenmeier saw Heidi she was not very pleased, as she thought Heidi would be far too young for Clara. And when she discovered that Heidi could neither read nor write, she was furious. But Dete explained that Heidi was a bright child and would learn quickly. Then she said goodbye to Heidi and left.

Fraulein Rottenmeier did not approve of Heidi's name, and insisted on calling her Adelheid. But Clara was delighted with her new friend. At supper time, Heidi was pleased to see a soft white roll on her plate, and she slipped the roll into her pocket. Sebastian, the butler, smiled when he saw this, but said nothing.

Fraulein Rottenmeier told Heidi that she must never speak to the servants as if they were friends. Then she told Heidi all the other things she must and must not do. Poor Heidi was so tired after her long journey to the city that she fell asleep at the supper table! Fraulein Rottenmeier was shocked. How could the child be so rude? But Clara thought it the most entertaining meal she had ever had.

An eventful day

When Heidi woke up the next morning she found herself lying in a high white bed in a large room. She blinked and rubbed her eyes, trying to think where she was.

Suddenly she remembered – this was Frankfurt. At once she jumped out of bed and dressed herself, then crept behind the long heavy curtains to look outside. But all she could see was the house across the street. There were no green fields or trees.

Since Clara couldn't go to school, a teacher gave her lessons at home, and Heidi was going to share those lessons. After breakfast, she went into the schoolroom with Clara.

Halfway through the morning, Fraulein Rottenmeier was startled to hear a loud

commotion in the schoolroom. She rushed in to find the whole room in an uproar. Books, papers and pens were scattered over the floor. Ink was spilled everywhere. And there was no sign of Heidi.

'What is the meaning of this disgusting mess?' cried Fraulein Rottenmeier. 'And where is Adelheid?'

'Please don't be cross,' pleaded Clara. 'Heidi heard a carriage in the street and she rushed downstairs to look at it. In her excitement she knocked everything off the table.'

Fraulein Rottenmeier hurried downstairs, and found Heidi standing in the open doorway, looking out into the street.

'I thought I heard the wind howling through the pine trees,' was all Heidi could say, sadly.

'Pine trees! What nonsense!' exclaimed Fraulein Rottenmeier. 'Do you think we live in a wood? Come upstairs at once.'

Poor Heidi! How she longed to run outside and see trees and mountains again. She felt like a prisoner, shut up in the big house. That afternoon, while Clara rested in her room, Heidi crept downstairs and opened the front door. She stepped into the street and was soon completely lost.

Then she saw a boy about the same age as herself. His clothes were dirty and ragged and he was playing a barrel organ. Heidi asked him where she could go to see the mountains, and the boy took her to a church with a very high tower.

The church caretaker let Heidi climb upstairs to the top of the tower. The city of Frankfurt stretched all around as far as the eye could see, but there were no mountains.

Heidi was very disappointed. Then, as she made her way downstairs, she caught sight of a large basket under the sloping roof of the church. The basket was full of kittens! To Heidi's delight, the caretaker gave her two of the tiny creatures. She put one in each pocket, then found her way back to Clara's house.

Heidi rang the doorbell and Sebastian let her in. He told her to be quick, as everyone was at dinner and Fraulein Rottenmeier was extremely angry.

'Adelheid!' began Fraulein Rottenmeier, as
soon as Heidi took her place at the table, 'You
have behaved very badly. How dare you leave
the house without permission?'

'Miaow!'

'What, Adelheid! You are rude as well as
naughty! I warn you!'

'I didn't...' began Heidi in distress. 'Miaow!
Miaow!'

'That will do!' snapped Fraulein Rottenmeier.
'Leave the room at once!'

'But I didn't...' stammered poor Heidi.
'Miaow! Miaow!'

22

'Heidi,' said Clara, 'why do you keep saying "Miaow"? It really is very rude of you.'

'It isn't me – it's the kittens,' explained Heidi, almost in tears.

'What! Cats!' screamed Fraulein Rottenmeier. 'Sebastian! Remove the disgusting animals at once!' And with that she fled to her room and locked the door. She hated cats more than anything.

Then Sebastian promised to hide the kittens where Fraulein Rottenmeier would never find them, and the two girls spent many happy hours playing with their pets in a dusty attic room.

Heidi is homesick

As each day passed, Heidi talked of nothing but Peter and the goats, her grandfather and the mountains. She was becoming more and more unhappy.

'I must go home tomorrow,' she would say each day. But Clara would persuade her to stay, saying, 'Just wait until Papa comes home!'

But still Heidi longed to return to the mountains. And she had saved so many rolls for Grandmother!

Then one afternoon the thought of her beloved mountains was too much for Heidi. She took the rolls from the back of her wardrobe, where she had hidden them, put on her old straw hat and shawl, and set off for home. But

Fraulein Rottenmeier saw her and marched her back to the house. She couldn't believe her ears when Heidi told her how homesick she was.

'How could you leave this beautiful house?' she demanded. 'Have you ever been treated better or had so many servants to look after you? You are an ungrateful little girl.'

With a heavy heart, Heidi put the rolls, the shawl and the old straw hat back in the wardrobe. Then Fraulein Rottenmeier said it was time Heidi had some new clothes. That old red shawl and straw hat had to go.

She pulled the shawl out of the wardrobe and discovered the pile of rolls hidden there.

'What is the meaning of this?' she demanded. 'Take that stale bread out of there at once – and I will throw away the old straw hat.'

'No, no!' screamed Heidi. 'Not the hat! And the rolls are for Grandmother!'

But Fraulein Rottenmeier would not listen. Heidi threw herself into Clara's arms, sobbing as though her heart would break.

Clara said, 'Heidi, please don't cry! I will give you as many rolls as you want when you go home, and they will be soft and fresh.'

It was a long time before Heidi could stop crying, but Clara's words had comforted her a little.

At bedtime, Heidi had a lovely surprise. There, hidden under the bedcover, was her old straw hat! Sebastian had rescued it and kept it for her. Heidi hugged it with delight, then wrapped it in a handkerchief and hid it right at the back of her wardrobe.

Clara's father and grandmother

A few days later there was great excitement in the house because Herr Sesemann, Clara's father, had returned.

Fraulein Rottenmeier told him at once that Heidi was not at all suitable as a companion for his daughter. Herr Sesemann listened to her, then replied that Clara was very happy with her new friend. He felt that his daughter's happiness was more important than anything else.

Herr Sesemann was at home for only a short time before setting off on his travels again. However, the day after he left, a letter arrived from Clara's grandmother to say that she was going to arrive the very next day. Clara was overjoyed.

Clara's grandmother had twinkling eyes and wore a lacy frill over her white hair. Heidi called her 'Madam' to start with, because Fraulein Rottenmeier had told her to do so. But the old lady smiled and said Heidi should call her Grandmamma, as Clara did.

One afternoon while Clara was resting, Grandmamma called Heidi to her room to show her a book with beautiful pictures in it. Suddenly tears streamed down Heidi's cheeks as she looked at a picture of a lovely green pasture. A shepherd leant on his stick, sheep and goats grazed peacefully, and everything was bathed in a golden light from the setting sun.

Grandmamma took Heidi's hand gently. 'Come, come, child! Don't cry! Does the picture remind you of something? There is a beautiful story about it and I am going to read it to you. So dry your eyes and be happy again.'

Grandmamma had been surprised to hear that Heidi could neither read nor write, and she began to read to her every afternoon. She promised that Heidi could keep the book when she had learned to read for herself. Heidi felt much happier when she was with Grandmamma, but she was still very homesick. She knew now that she couldn't go home whenever she wanted to, as Dete had promised.

As the days went by she lost her appetite, and grew thin and pale. At night she lay awake and longed to be back in the mountains. When at last she fell asleep she dreamt of the crimson snowfield in the setting sun. Each time she woke up and realised she was still in the big bed in Frankfurt, she would weep quietly, her face pressed into the pillow so that no one should hear.

Grandmamma noticed how pale Heidi had become, but when she asked what was wrong, Heidi would not tell her. She didn't want Grandmamma to think she was ungrateful. Then Grandmamma told Heidi that if she had any troubles she should pray to God for his help. So Heidi prayed every night, begging with all her heart to be allowed to return to her grandfather.

One day Clara's teacher was amazed to discover that Heidi could read at last. That evening Grandmamma gave Heidi the beautiful picture book, just as she had promised. Before she went to bed Heidi read aloud to Clara and Grandmamma, and from that day on, her greatest pleasure was to read the stories, over and over again.

*　　*　　*

The house is haunted

The day came when Grandmamma had to leave. Heidi and Clara felt very sad as they watched her carriage drive away.

That evening, Heidi read aloud to Clara. The story was a sad tale about a grandmother who was dying. Heidi at once thought of Peter's grandmother and burst into tears. Clara tried to explain that it was only a story, but Heidi couldn't stop crying. She kept thinking about Peter's grandmother, and her own dear grandfather, too. What if they became ill and died? She might never see them again.

Autumn and winter passed and the spring sun
shone on the wall of the house opposite. Heidi
knew it would soon be time for Peter to take
the goats up to the pasture. She thought of the
flowers glittering in the sunshine and the
mountains turning crimson in the setting sun.
And every night she cried into her pillow as
though her heart would break.

Then one morning something very strange
happened. When Sebastian came downstairs he
found the front door standing wide open. At
first he thought a burglar had been in the house,
but nothing was missing and no damage had
been done.

The next day the same thing happened, so Sebastian sat up all night in a small room next to the hall. Just as the clock struck one, a sudden breeze blew out the candle. Sebastian rushed into the hall. The front door was wide open, and there on the stairs stood a ghostly white figure. He blinked — and the figure vanished.

When Fraulein Rottenmeier heard what had happened, she wrote to Herr Sesemann, telling him that there was a ghost in the house, and begging him to come home.

Herr Sesemann returned at once. That night he asked his friend, Doctor Classen, to wait with him in the small room by the hall. Just as the clock struck one, they heard the front door opening. With pistols at the ready, they stepped into the hall. Moonlight streamed through the open door and fell on a small ghostly figure.

'Who is there?' demanded the doctor. Both men moved slowly forwards, and suddenly the figure gave a cry. It was Heidi, trembling and blinking in the light!

'What are you doing here, my child?' asked Herr Sesemann in surprise.

'I – I don't know,' whispered Heidi. Her feet were bare, and all she had on was her little white nightgown. She was shivering with cold as well as fright.

The doctor put his pistol down and carried Heidi gently upstairs to bed. 'Everything is all right,' he said in a kind voice. 'Now tell me where you wanted to go.'

'Every night I dream I'm with Grandfather,' replied Heidi, 'and I run quickly and open the cottage door to see the pine trees. But when I wake up, I am still in Frankfurt.'

Then the doctor asked Heidi all about her grandfather and his cottage. As she told him, the tears gushed from her eyes and her whole body shook with sobs. The doctor stroked her head. 'Try to sleep now,' he said gently. 'In the morning, everything will be all right.'

He went downstairs and told Herr Sesemann that Heidi had been sleepwalking because she was so homesick. The only thing that would help would be for her to return to her grandfather at once.

Back to the Alm

The next morning, Heidi could scarcely believe that she was on her way home at last. It was a sad day for Clara, but her father promised that she could visit Heidi the following year.

The journey passed quickly and it wasn't long before Heidi arrived at Grandmother's cottage. She took twelve soft white rolls from her basket and piled them on the old lady's lap.

Grandmother was delighted with the rolls, but she was even more delighted to have Heidi at her side once more. Then Heidi set off for her grandfather's cottage, promising to return the next day.

The sun was setting as Heidi climbed the steep path, and she stopped to gaze at the wonderful sight that lay before her. She had not

remembered, even in her dreams, how beautiful
it was. The mountains rose like flames above
the rose-coloured snowfield. Far below stretched
the valley, and all around everything glittered
and sparkled.

At last Heidi reached the cottage, and found
Grandfather sitting outside, smoking his pipe.
Heidi threw herself into his arms, crying,
'Grandfather! Grandfather!'

For a minute or two, the old man couldn't speak. His eyes were wet with tears, which he brushed away roughly with the back of his hand. He lifted his granddaughter onto his knee and kissed her. Heidi gave him a leather money bag and a letter from Herr Sesemann. When Grandfather had read the letter, he gave the money bag to Heidi. 'I have no need for money,' he said. 'You keep it, Heidi.' Heidi said she would use the money to buy fresh rolls every day for Grandmother.

That night Heidi slept peacefully for the first time in nearly a year. It was so wonderful to be in her little bed of hay!

The following Sunday Grandfather and Heidi
got up early and walked down to the village.
They were going to church, because Heidi had
told Grandfather how Grandmamma had taught
her to say her prayers every day. The villagers
were amazed to see the Alm Uncle in church.

After the service, Heidi and her grandfather
went to the pastor's house, where the pastor
greeted the Alm Uncle like an old friend. Then
Grandfather told him that he had decided to
move to the village for the winter, so that Heidi
could go to school every day. Thanks to Heidi,
Grandfather was no longer the fierce old Alm
Uncle who hated everybody.

Winter in Dorfli

As soon as the first snows fell, Heidi and her grandfather shut up the cottage. They moved into a big old house in Dorfli, and Heidi started going to school.

Heidi liked her new home. The house had been empty for many years, and part of it was in ruins, but Grandfather had come many times during the autumn to make it comfortable. In one corner of the biggest room stood a huge stove. It was decorated with blue and white tiles and there was a wooden bench all around it. In the space between the stove and the wall Grandfather had built a high wooden bed for Heidi.

Heidi liked going to school as well, and the winter passed happily for her. She missed seeing Grandmother however. Then one day the snow froze hard, and Heidi was able to walk up to Peter's cottage. It was very cold, and Grandmother was trying to keep warm in bed, an old grey shawl wrapped round her shoulders.

Heidi read some of Grandmother's favourite hymns.

'If only Peter could read to me,' sighed the old lady, 'my days wouldn't be so dreary.'

So, for the next few weeks, Heidi spent every spare moment teaching Peter to read. What a lovely surprise Grandmother had, when her grandson read aloud to her for the very first time!

News from Clara

Spring came and the snows melted away. It was time to leave Dorfli and return to the cottage. How wonderful it was to be back on the Alm again!

Clara had written to Heidi, to say that she and Grandmamma would be coming to the mountains very soon. Sure enough, one sunny morning, a strange procession could be seen making its way up the steep mountain path. In front was Grandmamma, riding a fine horse. Then came two men carrying Clara in a special chair. They were followed by another man who was pushing Clara's empty wheelchair.

When the visitors reached the cottage, Grandfather and Grandmamma greeted each other warmly. They had heard so much about each other that they felt like old friends.

Grandfather lifted Clara gently into her wheelchair, and the men returned to the village.

Clara and Grandmamma were entranced by everything they saw. They spent a wonderful day on the Alm, but all too soon it was time to leave.

Then Grandfather suggested that Clara should stay for a few weeks. The pure mountain air and the simple food would do her good. Grandmamma agreed at once. She set off on her own, promising to write very soon.

Grandfather made Clara a lovely soft bed in the hayloft, and that night she lay next to Heidi, gazing at the stars. She had never been so happy.

As each day passed, Clara became stronger. Her cheeks glowed with health and her eyes sparkled with happiness.

The only person who wasn't happy was Peter. Heidi was spending all her time with Clara, and he hardly ever saw her.

An unexpected event

Every morning, when Grandfather lifted Clara into her wheelchair, he made her stand with both feet on the ground. At first she cried out in pain, but each day she stood for a little longer.

Clara was longing to see the pasture, so one morning Grandfather put her wheelchair ready outside the cottage, before going inside to make breakfast.

Just then Peter came by with the goats. The sight of the wheelchair made him very angry. He thought that if the wheelchair disappeared, Clara would have to go back to Frankfurt, and he would have Heidi all to himself again. Without another thought, he pushed the wheelchair with all his might. It rolled down the mountainside and smashed into pieces on the rocks far below. Peter laughed loudly, then ran all the way to the pasture.

When Grandfather brought Clara outside he couldn't think what had happened to the wheelchair. But it didn't stop Clara from going to the pasture. Grandfather carried her all the way there. Peter's heart sank when he saw her, but he said nothing.

Clara and Heidi spent a wonderful day on the pasture. Heidi wanted Clara to see the most beautiful flowers, which grew at the other side of the pasture. Clara couldn't see them from where she was sitting, and Heidi called Peter to help her to lift Clara. At first, Peter refused, but at last he agreed to help.

Peter and Heidi held Clara tightly round her waist, and Heidi told Clara to take a step. Clara tried, and cried out in pain. But the second step she took didn't hurt so much. Then, almost before she knew it, she had taken several steps, with Peter and Heidi still helping her. She was so excited she could hardly speak. To think that she could walk!

When Grandfather returned, he was delighted to hear that Clara had taken a few steps. But he didn't want her to get too tired, so he carried her all the way home.

The next day Clara took a few more steps, this time with Grandfather helping her. Heidi sat down and wrote to Grandmamma, inviting her to the Alm once more. But she didn't tell her that Clara had started to walk. It was to be a surprise.

Promises to meet again

When Grandmamma arrived, she was astonished to see Clara sitting on the bench outside the cottage.

'Why, Clara, is it really you?' she cried. 'Your cheeks are so rosy and round! And you're not in your wheelchair! I hardly recognised you.' Then she gasped in disbelief as Clara got up, and with Heidi's help, walked slowly towards her.

The old lady hugged her granddaughter, then she hugged Heidi. She looked across at the Alm Uncle, tears of happiness in her eyes.

'How can I ever thank you?' she cried. But Grandfather said it was the fresh air and the goats' milk that had helped Clara most.

Grandmamma wanted to send a telegram to Clara's father to come at once. She wrote the telegram down, and Heidi gave it to Peter to take to the Post Office.

However, Clara's father was already on his
way to the Alm. He had finished his business
and longed to see his daughter again, so he
made the long journey to Switzerland. He was
climbing up the mountain path when he met
Peter and asked if he was on the right path.
Peter thought Herr Sesemann must be a
policeman from Frankfurt who had come to take
him away for breaking the wheelchair, and he
was frightened. The boy turned and ran,
dropping the telegram in his haste.

When at last Herr Sesemann found his way to
the cottage, he saw a tall, fair girl with rosy
cheeks walking towards him. She was leaning
on a smaller, dark haired girl. He stopped and
stared at them.

'Papa, don't you know me?' asked Clara. 'Have I changed so much?'

At once, Herr Sesemann rushed to kiss his daughter. 'Yes, you have changed indeed! Is it possible? Can this be my Clara?'

He turned to Grandfather and shook his hand warmly. 'How can I ever repay you?' he asked.

At that moment, Heidi caught sight of Peter, hiding behind the pine trees. Peter was terrified. He was sure the man from Frankfurt was going to take him away. Grandmamma called him to her, and asked him, very gently, what was the matter. She spoke so kindly that Peter blurted out the truth at once. He told her how he had pushed the wheelchair down the mountainside, because he was jealous of Clara. And he told her that he had lost the telegram.

Grandmamma didn't scold him. She said she understood how he felt, and she wanted to give him a present from Frankfurt. He could have anything he wished.

Peter couldn't believe his ears. After thinking for a while, he said he would like a penny. Grandmamma laughed. Then she gave him a whole lot of pennies — as many as he could hold in his hand.

Peter had never seen so much money in his life. He put it carefully in his pocket, then ran all the way home, laughing and shouting at the top of his voice.

Herr Sesemann asked Heidi if there was anything she would like. Heidi replied that she would like to give her big bed in Frankfurt to Peter's grandmother.

Herr Sesemann promised to send the bed as soon as possible. Then Heidi took Grandmamma to meet Grandmother.

The hours passed quickly, and all too soon it was time to say goodbye. Clara didn't want to leave the Alm, but her father promised that she could return every year.

Heidi and her grandfather stood and waved to their friends until they disappeared from sight. Everything was bathed in a rosy glow from the setting sun as, hand in hand, they walked back to the cottage on the Alm.